D1103889

Esther K. Meeks

THE
Curious
Cow

ILLUSTRATED BY MEL PEKARSKY

Follett Publishing Company   Chicago   New York

Library of Congress Catalog Card Number: 60-13351

FIFTH PRINTING   TLA 1650

Katy was Farmer Green's cow.

She was a pretty cow.

She gave good milk.

Farmer Green and Mrs. Green
liked Katy.

Katy was a good cow.

She stood still while Farmer Green milked her.

She never hurt anyone.

Katy was a good cow in every way but one.

Katy was too curious.

She always wanted to find out
about the grass in the neighbor's field.

It looked greener.

Was it better grass?

Katy wanted to know.

She saw a place to go through
the fence.

The grass was just the same as
Farmer Green's grass.

Katy liked it better anyway.

But Farmer Green did not like it.

"Katy!" he said. "You bad cow!"

Another day Katy saw a garden
gate open.

She could see pretty green plants
in the garden.

Were they as good to eat
as they looked?

Katy wanted to know.

The plants were good.

Katy liked them.

But Farmer Green did not

like it.

"My carrots! My tomatoes!

Bad Katy!" said Farmer Green.

One day Katy saw something

white flying over the fence.

Was it good to eat?

Katy wanted to know.

She tried to eat the white things.

She tried all of them.

Katy did not like them.

Mrs. Green did not like it
when she saw Katy.
"Oh! Oh!" said Mrs. Green.
"Look! My wash!
Bad, bad Katy!"

But she was good most of the time.

She was bad only when she was curious.

Farmer Green and Mrs. Green still

liked Katy.

One day Katy was in the yard.

It was a warm day.

The door to the house was open.

What was on the other side of the door?

Katy wanted to know.

Katy went up the steps.

The door was just big enough for
Katy to get through.

Katy was in the kitchen.

Katy moved her head.

BANG! went a pan.

Katy moved her tail.

CRASH! went some glasses.

Mrs. Green came running.

17

"Help! Help!" said Mrs. Green.

"Katy is in the kitchen!"

Farmer Green came running.

"Bad Katy!" said Farmer Green.

"A cow should not be in the kitchen!

Get out! Get out!"

Farmer Green led Katy through the doorway.

He tried to lead her down the steps.

But Katy just looked at him with her big sad eyes.

Katy seemed to say,

"I can go up the steps.

But I can not go down the steps."

Poor Farmer Green!

He pushed and he pulled.

But Katy could not go down
the steps.

Farmer Green did not know
what to do.

Then he had an idea.

He put big boards on the steps.

He led Katy to the boards.

Katy could go down the boards.

"Good Katy!" Farmer Green said.

"But please stay out of the kitchen!"

One day Farmer Green could not
find Katy.

Mrs. Green could not find Katy.

They looked everywhere.

In the barn.

In the field.

In the neighbors' fields.

But no one could find Katy.

Then Farmer Green heard the dog bark.

He followed the dog.

He heard something. "Moo! Moo!"

It was Katy. "Moo! Moo!"

But where was she?

Farmer Green looked.

There was Katy.

She was in a big hole.

Katy could not get out.

She was sad.

Farmer Green was sad too.

He did not know how to get
Katy out.

The neighbors came.

They tried to put a rope around

Katy and pull her out.

That did not help.

They tried to dig Katy out.

But the dirt was too soft.

Policemen came.

The fire department came.

Everyone tried to help Katy.

Then someone had an idea.

The firemen pumped water into

the hole.

As the water got higher,

Katy began to swim.

Soon she was high enough for

the men to pull her out.

After that Katy was not so curious.

She stayed where she belonged

and was always good Katy.

THE CURIOUS COW

Reading Level: Level One. *The Curious Cow* has a total vocabulary of 178 words. It has been tested in first grade classes, where it was read with ease.

Uses of This Book: Reading for fun. Kindness to animals is emphasized, and children will be amused by the problems Farmer Green has with his curious cow.

Word List

All of the 178 words used in *The Curious Cow* are listed. Regular plurals *(-s)* and regular verb forms *(-s, -ed, -ing)* of words already on the list are not listed separately, but the endings are given in parentheses after the word.

5	Katy	6	stood	7	always		know
	was		still		wanted		saw
	Farmer		while		to		place
	Green('s)		her		find		go
	cow		never		out		through
	she		hurt		about		fence
	a		anyone		the	8	just
	pretty		in		grass		same
	gave		every		neighbor's		as
	good		way		field		anyway
	milk(ed)		but		it		did
	and		one		look(ed)		not
	Mrs.		too		green(er)		he
	like(d)		curious		better		said

you
bad

9 another
day
garden
gate
open
could
see
plants
were
they
eat

10 them
my
carrots
tomatoes

11 something
white
flying
over
tried
things
all
of

12 when
oh
wash

13 most
time
only

14 yard
warm
door
house
what
on
other
side

15 went
up
steps
big
enough
for
get
kitchen

16 moved
head
bang
pan

17 tail
crash
some
glasses
came
running

18 help
is
should
be

19 led
doorway
lead
down
at
him
with
sad
eyes
seemed
say
I
can

20 poor
pushed
pull (ed)
do

21 then
had
an
idea
put
boards
please
stay (ed)

22 everywhere
barn
no

23 heard
dog
bark
followed

moo
where

24 there
hole
how

25 rope
around
that

26 dig
dirt
soft
policemen
fire
department
everyone

27 someone
firemen
pumped
water
into

28 got
high (er)
began
swim
soon
men

29 after
so
belonged

The Follett BEGINNING-TO-READ Books

Purpose of the Beginning-to-Read Books: To provide easy-to-read materials that will appeal to the interests of primary children. Careful attention is given to vocabulary load and sentence length, but the first criterion is interest to children.

Reading Levels: These books are written at three reading levels, indicated by one, two, or three dots beneath the *Beginning-to-Read* symbol on the back cover. *Level One* books can be read by first grade children in the last half of the school year. As children increase their reading ability they will be able to enjoy *Level Two* books. And as they grow further in their reading ability they will progress to *Level Three* books. Some first grade children will read *Level Two* and *Level Three* books. Many third graders, and even some fourth graders, will read and enjoy *Level One* and *Level Two* books, as well as *Level Three* books. The range of interest of *Beginning-to-Read* books stretches far beyond their reading level.

Use of the Beginning-to-Read Books: Because of their high interest and readability, these books are ideal for independent reading by primary children—at school, in the library, and at home. The books may also be incorporated into the basic reading program to develop children's interests, expand their vocabularies, and improve word-attack skills. It has been suggested that they might serve as the foundation for a skillfully directed reading program. Many *Beginning-to-Read* books correlate with the social studies, science, and other subject fields. All will help children grow in the language arts. Children will read the *Beginning-to-Read* books with confidence, with success, and with real enjoyment.